Mr. Tazaki, the owner of the center, called in Scooby-Doo and his Mystery, Inc. pals to solve the curse of the samurai ghost.

"Man, Japan has pretty good food," Shaggy said. "Like, I can't wait to bite into these peanut butter and cucumber sushi rolls."

In Japan, on the slopes below Mt. Fuji, workers were busy building a new children's sports center when they heard an eerie horn blaring. *AAWOOO!*

"Beware! Flee or be cursed!" growled a samurai ghost on horseback. "This is sacred land!"

visit us at www.abdopublishing.com

Reinforced library bound edition published in 2010 by Spotlight, a division of the ABDO Group, 8000 West 78th Street, Edina, Minnesota 55439. Spotlight produces high-quality reinforced library bound editions for schools and libraries. Published by agreement with Warner Bros.—A Time Warner Company. The stories, characters, and incidents mentioned are entirely fictional. All rights reserved. Used under authorization.

For Lillian and Roger Segar.
Thanks for giving me the best gift ever!

Printed in the United States of America, Melrose Park, Illinois.
092009
012010

Special thanks to Duendes del Sur for cover and interior illustrations.

Library of Congress Cataloging-in-Publication Data

McCann, Jesse Leon.
  Scooby-Doo and the samurai ghost / by Jesse Leon McCann ; [cover and interior illustrations, Dan Davis]. -- Reinforced library bound ed.
      p. cm.
  ISBN 978-1-59961-679-7
  I. Davis, Dan W. II. Scooby-Doo (Television program) III. Title.
  PZ7.M47835Scp 2010
  [Fic]--dc22
                                                                                                          2009031241

All Spotlight books are reinforced library binding and manufactured in the United States of America.

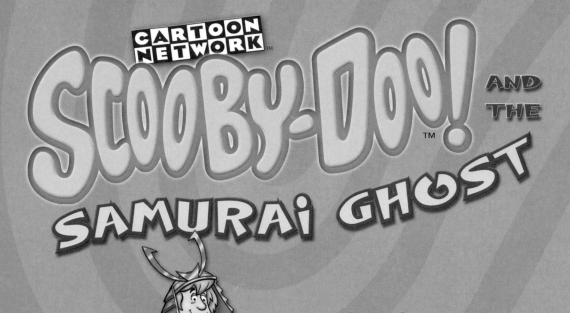

SCOOBY-DOO! AND THE

SAMURAI GHOST

Spotlight

"Reah, reah!" Scooby licked his lips hungrily. "Rushi rolls."

Before they could eat, Scooby and Shaggy came face-to-face with a godzilla of a monster—or so they thought.

At a temple near the construction site, Mr. Tazaki introduced the gang to his vice president, Jiro.

"No one will work because of the samurai's curse," Jiro said sadly.

6

AWOOO!

"Didn't you say a horn blew right before the samurai attacked?" Daphne asked.

"Jinkies! It's coming from the cherry orchard," Velma added. "We'd better check it out."

"Roh-no!" Scooby cried as the samurai ghost charged into view.

"You have brought the samurai curse upon yourselves!" the ghost roared. "Prepare to meet your doom!" With hands like steel, he karate-chopped his way through. *KRAK! KRAK! CHOP!*

"Zoinks!" gulped Shaggy. "The only meeting I want is my feet meeting the ground. Come on Scoob, let's get out of here."

Shaggy and Scooby scrambled away, barely staying out of the samurai ghost's reach. They were running so fast, they didn't notice until too late that they were heading for a cliff. Over they went.

"Ruh-no, Raggy!" called Scooby.
"Like, look out below!" cried Shaggy.
SPLASH! Shaggy and Scooby landed in the river.
Woozy from their fall, they floated along.

Eventually, a pair of hands grabbed them and a voice said, "These are two of the strangest fish I've ever caught."

The fisherman's name was Oki. He knew all about samurai, because his father had been one.

"Yes, the samurai's curse is real," Oki said. "You are in great danger."

"Ruh-oh!" Scooby gulped. He and Shaggy were afraid he'd say that.

The next morning, the gang decided to set out early to look for clues. They started in the bamboo orchard. "Look at this," Daphne announced. "It's an insurance policy, but it's written in Japanese so I can't read it."

"We'll translate it later," Velma said. "In the meantime, there's something odd about these tracks."

Luckily, Fred had a plan and the workers agreed to help. By late in the day, they had built a stage for the gang to put on a show.

"This Kabuki show should be loud enough to get the ghost's attention," Velma said as Shaggy and Scooby danced around the stage Kabuki-style.

According to plan, the samurai ghost crashed onto the scene. "Zoinks! It's that sneaky spirit!" Shaggy yelled. "Everybody run!" Nobody needed to be told twice, least of all Scooby-Doo.

"Take that!" Fred cried as he jumped out of the bushes and ran toward the samurai with a net. But it was of no use—the samurai knocked the net away easily with his pole.

"Fool!" growled the samurai. "I have vanquished a thousand ninjas!"

With the samurai closing in behind them, the gang once again found themselves at the cliff.

"Jinkies!" cried Velma dropping her glasses.

Unable to see, Velma had no idea that the samurai ghost was heading right for her. Scooby wasn't about to let her get run over by a horse. He made the scariest face he could think of— just like the Godzilla balloon monster, "*GRRRRR!*"

It worked. The horse stopped short and the samurai ghost flew over the cliff.

"Help! I can't swim," cried the samurai ghost in the river. Velma got Oki to row her out to the samurai ghost. She took off its mask, "Just as we thought. It's Mr. Tazaki. We knew they weren't real ghosts because the horseshoe prints weren't the kind a samurai's steed would wear."

And this insurance contract Mr. Tazaki dropped gave him away—insurance that would pay him a lot of money if the sports center never got built. Bringing to life the curse of the samurai ghost was supposed to make sure it never did."

"It would have worked, too, if I hadn't called you kids and that dog," Mr. Tazaki grumbled.

Mystery solved, the local children would have a new sports center after all. Thanks to Mystery, Inc., and a dog named Scooby-Doo.

"Rooby-Dooby-Doo!"